SAIL AWAY

Donald Crews

Greenwillow Books / New York

To the _Seabiscuit_,
captain and crew,
and to being here
to tell this tale

The full-color illustrations were created
with Dr. Martin's Concentrated Water Colors
applied with brush and airbrush. The text
type is Akzidenz Grotesk Bold Italic.

HarperCollins Publishers,
195 Broadway, New
York, NY 10007.
Manufactured in China.
First Edition
15 SCP 20 19 18 17 16 15 14 13 12 11

Library of Congress
Cataloging-in-Publication Data

Crews, Donald.
Sail away / by Donald Crews.
p.   cm.
Summary: A family takes an
enjoyable trip in their sailboat
and watches the weather
change throughout the day.
ISBN 0-688-11053-3 (trade).
ISBN 0-688-11054-1 (lib. bdg.)
ISBN 0-688-17517-1 (pbk.)
[1. Sailing—Fiction.]
I. Title.   PZ7.C8682Sai
1995   [E]—dc20   94-6004
CIP   AC

**A perfect
day for
sailing.**

We row the dinghy out to our sailboat.

**Everything ready,
we motor from our mooring.**

p u t t . . . p u t t . . . p u t t . . .

putt...putt...putt...
Under the bridge.
putt...putt...putt...

putt...putt...putt...
**Past the lighthouse.
Motor off.** *putt...* **Sails up ...**

Wind's up...

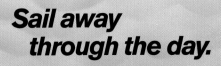

Sail away through the day.

**Sailing, sailing.
Clear skies turn
cloudy and gray.**

Gray skies darken.
Seas swell.

Darker skies, higher seas…
Angry seas.
"Shorten sails!"

Sails down, we turn for home.

**Calm again at last.
The sun is setting
as we motor toward port.**

p u t t . . . p u t t . . . p u t t . . .

putt...putt...putt...
Past the lighthouse.
putt...putt...putt...

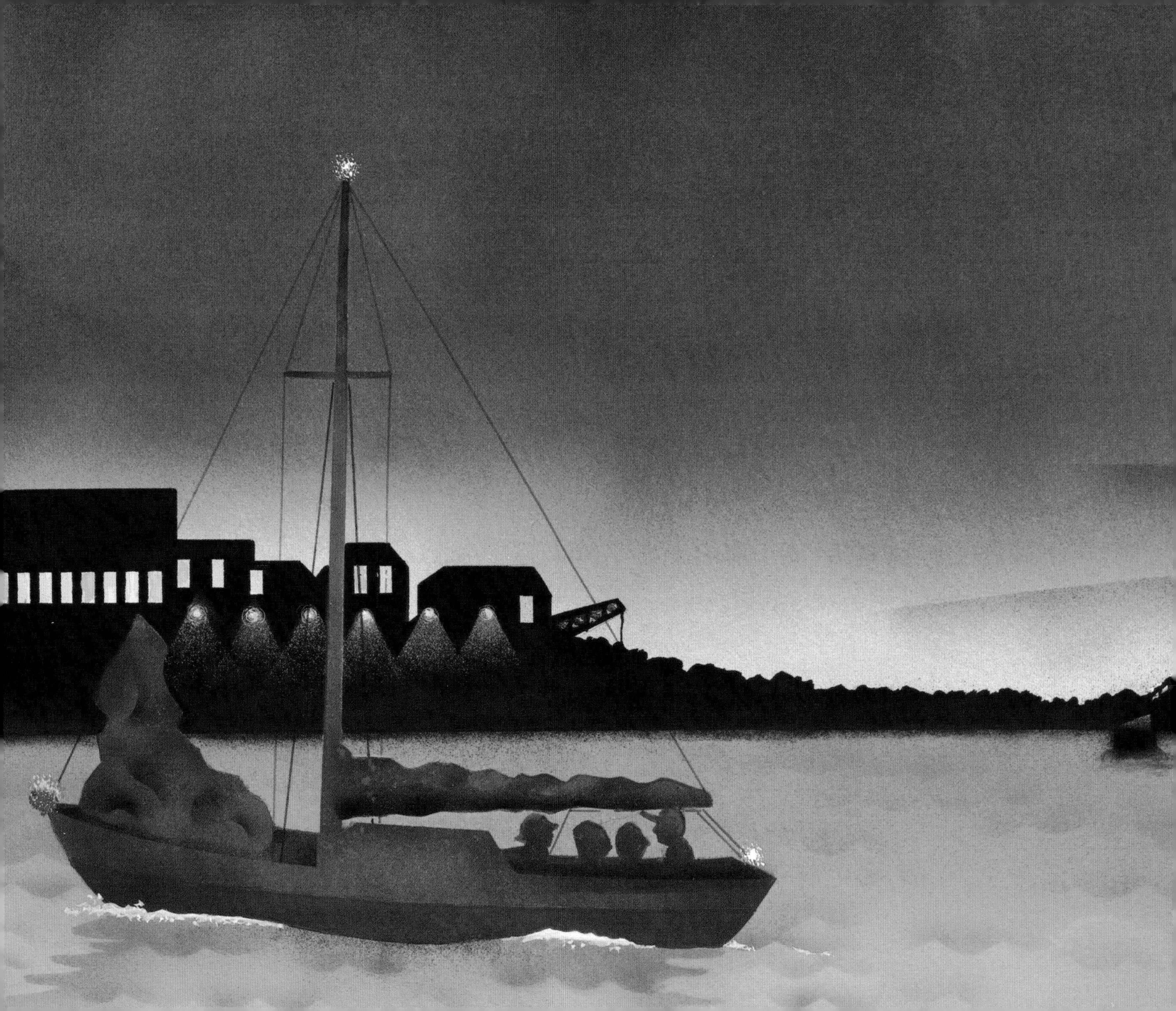

putt...putt...putt...
Under the bridge.
putt...putt...putt...

Moored!